CATHY CARSON

Healing Hoppy

A Story about Holistic Care and Kindness

Paisley,
You can and you will.
Cathy 2021

AKA Caitie the cat

Healing Hoppy

A Story about Holistic Care and Kindness

iUniverse books may be ordered through booksellers or by contacting:

iUniverse
1663 Liberty Drive
Bloomington, IN 47403
www.iuniverse.com
844-349-9409

ISBN: 978-1-5320-9111-7 (sc)
ISBN: 978-1-5320-9112-4 (e)

Library of Congress Control Number: 2021902950

Print information available on the last page.

iUniverse rev. date: 03/27/2021

Healing Hoppy

A Story about Holistic Care and Kindness

It was a beautiful, warm, sunny summer day on Frog Pond. The sky was painted a welcoming soft blue. The sun, a sparkling yellow, was shining down, warming the earth.

Hoppy the frog sat on a tree stump watching all the other frogs playing in the schoolyard. They were hopping over dried logs and playing hide-and-seek behind some bare bushes. Even though it was a lovely day, Hoppy just wasn't feeling like himself. He thought, *I don't even feel like hopping or singing my croaking songs. Even my favorite snacks that Mommy packed in my lunch tasted strange.*

He felt a little sad watching his friends play. They were all having so much fun, and he didn't even have the energy to hop.

After outside playtime, he was feeling tired, so he put his head on his desk and closed his eyes for a wee nap. His teacher, Miss Lucy, a brown and white long-eared jackrabbit, had noticed that Hoppy wasn't his usual cheerful self today in the schoolyard. She knew he liked to hop—maybe nearly as much as she did!

This is not like Hoppy at all, thought Miss Lucy. So she brought him to see the school nurse.

Nurse Florence, a friendly, furry red fox, said, "Hi, Hoppy. Miss Lucy tells me that you aren't feeling like yourself! Can I help you hop up onto the treatment table so I can have a better look at you?"

Hoppy agreed, and Nurse Florence helped him get up onto the table. Hoppy watched as she gathered some medical things from the office. Her bushy red tail swayed from side to side as she walked around the room.

She started by placing a long thin tube under his tongue to take his temperature. She called the tube a ther … thermome … thermometer. She listened to his breathing with a funny ear thing. She taught him that this was called steth … stethes … stethoscope.

After she'd finished examining Hoppy, Nurse Florence called Hoppy's mommy and said, "Hoppy isn't feeling like himself. He didn't want to eat his lunch today or even play with his friends in the schoolyard. His temperature is good, and his heart is beating with a normal lub dub, lub dub sound. But he seems to have lost his hoppity-hop."

Hoppy's mommy said, "Thank you for calling. We will go and see the doctor in the morning."

The next day, Hoppy's mommy took him to see Doctor Ben, a honey badger. That morning, Doctor Ben was out on a house call, so instead, Hoppy was seen by the holistic nurse, Caitie. Caitie was a spunky calico cat with white, orange, and black patches on her coat. She had striking soft blue eyes, just like the sky on a summer day.

Although Hoppy didn't like going to the doctor's office, he always felt calm with the holistic nurse. Holistic nurses take care of the body, mind, and spirit of their patients.

Caitie asked Hoppy questions about all kinds of things, like the foods he ate, how he slept, and if he was feeling sad or happy. She also asked him about his friends, his hobbies, and things that he didn't like. He thought to himself, *She listens to me with her ears and her heart. This makes me feel very calm.*

Hoppy's mommy told Caitie, "Hoppy has not been feeling like himself. He loves to hop but just doesn't seem interested lately. I have not heard him singing his croaking songs in the evenings!"

After asking if it was okay, Nurse Caitie looked at Hoppy's eyes, ears, and throat with a special light. He watched as she listened to his chest with a medical thing just like Nurse Florence had. He thought, *I know what that is called. It's a stethe … stethoscope.*

She also looked at his skin. She gently pushed on his belly and watched for his response. She used a small little medical hammer to gently tap on his knees and elbows, checking his muscles' reflexes.

As he sat quietly during the checkup, Hoppy thought to himself, *I'm not sure why everyone is making such a fuss. I just don't feel like hopping.*

"Your little boy is not feeling like himself and has lost his hoppity-hop," Nurse Caitie told Hoppy's mommy. "Let me speak with Dr. Ben so we can figure out how to help Hoppy be well."

The next day, Hoppy's mommy got a call from Nurse Caitie.

"Dr. Ben and I feel that Hoppy may be able to get his hoppity-hop back by moving upstream," Nurse Caitie said. "We know of a pond where little frogs are healthy and strong. Many of my holistic friends live at the pond and keep all the animals well. Each has a special healing gift that helps other creatures feel better when they are not feeling like themselves."

"Oh?" said Hoppy's mommy, surprised by this suggestion. She was sad to think of leaving their home, but she and Hoppy's daddy would do anything to help their little boy.

"The pond is clean," Nurse Caitie continued, "and the plants grow tall and green."

"The Healing Pond is surrounded by lovely-smelling flowers, tall cattails, and many other healing plants. My friends at the Healing Pond love living there. They tell me that their hearts feel peaceful and calm because everyone there is so caring and kind."

She added, "The animals play outdoors. Some play hide-and-seek behind the tall cattails, and others gather plants and herbs from the forest. The animals take care of the pond and the land. In return, the pond treats them well by offering a safe and healing place."

Hoppy's mommy seemed less sad knowing that they had hope for helping Hoppy. Then, Nurse Caitie asked to speak to Hoppy.

"Hoppy," said Nurse Caitie, "Dr. Ben, my holistic friends from the Healing Pond, and your mommy and daddy will choose some healing gifts to help you get your hoppity-hop back. We want to help your mind, body, and spirit be strong and happy. All little frogs should have tons of energy to hop, hop, and hop."

That evening after dinner, Hoppy's mommy and daddy went for a hop outside. After a few minutes of hopping, they sat on a log by Frog Pond to have a chat about Hoppy. The small pond near their home was not a healthy pond. The frogs could not swim in the water until it was cleaner. There were only a few bare plants around the pond. The plants were short, a bit yellow, and looked sad and wilted.

Some days, a nasty, worrisome smell came from Frog Pond. The land and the pond were not being well taken care of by the community. No new trees or plants were seeded. Those that were planted did not grow well or tall.

Leaving Hoppy's friends behind would be hard and moving to the Healing Pond might be sad at first, but they wanted more than anything for Hoppy to be well. They came back in the house and told Hoppy, "We are going to take a leap of faith! We are all going to move upstream to the Healing Pond to help you get your hoppity-hop back."

That night, as Hoppy lay in his bed tucked under his favorite soft green blanket, he thought, *Moving is going to be a bit scary, but my mommy and daddy always make good choices for me and keep me safe. I want to get my hoppity-hop back so that I can hop all day long.*

The next morning, after eating a light breakfast, they packed up their favorite things and hiked upstream to the Healing Pond. Hoppy carried a small bag over his shoulder. Inside were some of his favorite things, like his soft green blanket. Hoppy hopped slowly, already missing his friends and home.

His mommy saw that her little boy was lagging and told him that it was okay to feel sad. "It is always safe to tell your mommy and daddy how your heart is feeling. Mommy and Daddy have sad feelings sometimes too, and we have sometimes lost our hoppity-hop!"

The trail seemed to go on forever, winding to the left and then to the right. In his head, Hoppy kept thinking, *Are we there yet?*

As they got closer to the pond, Hoppy noticed lovely-smelling flowers in many bright colors all along the path. The water in the pond looked so clean and still. The trees and the soft blue sky were perfectly reflected on the lake, like they were staring into a mirror. Fish were jumping in and out of the water, chasing each other like they were playing a game of tag. Fast-moving red-winged dragonflies skimmed the surface of the water, turning right and then a sharp left.

Just like Nurse Caitie had said, there were cattails around the pond, standing tall and proud. A gentle breeze made them sway back and forth. Hoppy thought, *That would be a good place to hide for hide-and-seek with my new friends*. The pretty flowers and the tall cattails made him smile. Even though he was missing his friends, his heart felt a little less sad.

When they arrived at the new pond, they were met by Stevie, a skunk. She had a furry black and white coat and a long, curly tail. A white stripe went from the top of her back to the tip of her tail. Hoppy wasn't too sure about skunks, but he knew that his mommy and daddy would keep him safe.

After they all said a friendly hello, Stevie said, "Welcome to the Healing Pond!"

Hoppy's mommy said, "The holistic nurse, Caitie, told us all about her friends with healing gifts. She said that coming to the Healing Pond could help Hoppy get his taste for food and his hoppity-hop back."

Stevie nodded her head as Hoppy's mommy told her story. "My healing gift is aromatherapy," she said. "This is when you make nice-smelling oils from healing plants that help make you feel better and get stronger. I also make teas from the leaves and flowers of certain plants."

Stevie took a long serious look at Hoppy and then reached into her healing bag. She offered the family a bottle of ginger essential oil, a bottle of peppermint essential oil, and a packet of tea.

"Hoppy, you should breathe the smell of the oils in and out slowly for several minutes before you eat your food," she said. "This can help your belly feel better and help you feel hungry. I am also giving you some ginger tea to sip at bedtime. The tea can help your belly be calm when it is feeling stormy."

That evening, Hoppy's mommy went to the cupboard where she had stored the oils from aromatherapist Stevie. Mommy prepared the oils for Hoppy. Before dinner, Hoppy sat on the log seat in their new home and slowly breathed in and then out the lovely odor of the peppermint and ginger oils his mommy had put on a leaf for him to smell. He did this for several minutes.

When he was done with smelling the oils, his mommy made sure that he washed his hands very well. "Touching your eyes with oils still on your hands could sting," she told him. "For your safety, always ask Mommy or Daddy to help you with the oils and the tea."

For dinner, Hoppy's mommy made him a yummy salad with dandelions, kale, and spinach, as well as other healing plants from Nurse Caitie's garden. Nurse Caitie used the healing plants every day to help her stay strong. As a holistic nurse, she was always teaching her friends and patients how to be well and healthy.

Before Hoppy went off to bed, his mommy made him a hot cup of ginger tea. She was extra careful to make sure that the tea was cool enough for Hoppy to drink. Once he was all done drinking the tea, his mommy helped him get ready for bed.

As he snuggled under his favorite soft green blanket, he thought to himself, *My belly is happy from all the yummy healing foods and ginger tea. Snuggling with my blankie reminds me of my old home. I am starting to feel better and a little less sad!*

When Hoppy awoke the next morning, he noticed that his belly was happy and hungry. He decided that he liked his new friend, aromatherapist Stevie, and her healing gift of oils and plants. He told his mommy, "Skunks really aren't stinky, and they make some good-smelling oils and yummy teas!"

That afternoon, as they were hopping around the Healing Pond, they met another new friend, acupuncturist Penelope, a porcupine. She was a round rodent with sharp-looking quills, brown and grey in color. She shared that she had a healing gift called *acupuncture*.

"What is an acu ... acup ... acupunct ... acupuncturrrr ...?" Hoppy asked.

Penelope said, "This is an ancient type of healing. We can use it with our patients to help them get stronger. What I do is gently put tiny quills on an invisible map on the skin. The tiny quills are like small straws or needles that are put on different parts of the body. It doesn't hurt. This healing gift helps make our bodies strong by helping balance the invisible energy. It can help with ouches or when we lose our hoppity-hop."

She smiled at Hoppy and continued, "This healing gift also helps balance our mind, body, and spirit. I studied for many years how, why, and when to use acupuncture, and where on the body to place the tiny quills to help with healing. My patients often fall asleep on the special table when they get acupuncture because they get so relaxed."

"This sounds like a good thing to try to help Hoppy with his upset stomach," said Hoppy's mommy.

Hoppy was thinking, *I'm starting to get a little nervous about small little quills being placed on my body. Even though this is all new to me, I want to try, since it could help me get my hoppity-hop back!*

The next morning, Hoppy's mommy took him to visit Penelope the acupuncturist for a healing visit. Penelope asked them a few questions, looked at Hoppy's tongue, and then checked his pulse on his arm. She then had Hoppy lay on a special table. His mommy stayed in the room and sat in a chair nearby.

With loving kindness, Penelope placed a few very tiny quills on different parts of Hoppy's frog-body. This was to help his belly feel hungry and help with his hoppity-hop. Hoppy rested on the table and had a nice little nap.

His mommy chuckled, thinking that her little frog looked a bit like a porcupine with the tiny quills poking out from his skin. She was proud to see how brave her little Hoppy was as he tried this new healing gift.

When he woke up from his nap, he said, "Mommy, that was easy, and I'm feeling better!"

On the way home, Hoppy was hopping over small branches and some Christmas ferns growing from the forest floor. His mommy was happy to see that he was feeling better and to see him playing again.

When he got back home, Hoppy told his daddy, "Penelope the porcupine is a really friendly rodent! I was a little scared at first to try the acu ... *acupuncture*, but she was so friendly and kind that I knew that I could trust her." Hoppy was laughing to himself thinking, *Mommy must have thought that I kind of looked like a porcupine with those quills on my skin!*

After dinner, Hoppy's mommy made him more of the ginger tea. Hoppy sipped some of the tea that his friend Stevie had given him as a gift. He was feeling very happy that he kept meeting new friends who shared their healing gifts. In his heart, he felt the care and kindness coming from each of them. This made his heart feel all warm inside.

That night, lying in his bed, Hoppy watched the sky and the sparkling stars from his window in their tree-log house. Tucked under his soft green blanket, he felt very safe and quickly fell asleep. He dreamt of his old home, his friends, and Frog Pond. At first, he was a little sad, but then his heart reminded him of the warmth that it felt every time he met another one of Caitie the holistic nurse's friends with healing gifts.

Later that evening, his mommy and daddy went to check on Hoppy. He was snuggled in his bed, croaking in his sleep, which made them laugh. They smiled as they closed the door to his room. They were happy to see Hoppy with more of his hoppity-hop with each new healing gift that he received.

The next morning after breakfast, Hoppy and his daddy took a walk to the Healing Pond while his mommy sat on a nearby log sipping her morning tea. Hoppy's mommy was really enjoying some chamomile tea from Stevie. It helped keep her mind quiet and her heart peaceful. She sat quietly, listening to the birds. They seemed happy, singing their lovely songs to the warm morning sun.

Hoppy and his daddy were strolling along a well-traveled path when they heard a noise. Hoppy and his daddy stopped to explore the sound. As they listened, they heard a swooshing sound in the trees above them going back and forth from branch to branch. When they looked up, they saw a brown squirrel with a long furry tail balancing on the branch.

The squirrel stopped as he realized he had some admirers. He introduced himself: "Hi there. My name is Sam."

"My name is Hoppy, and this is my daddy," Hoppy said. Hoppy was very impressed at how fast Sam the squirrel moved in the trees and how well he could balance himself on the branches. "How do you do that?" he asked Sam. "You move like the wind!"

"Well, every day, I practice an energy healing called healing touch. I begin by finding a space near the pond to be quiet. Sometimes, I have lots of thoughts in my mind, so I just pay attention to my breathing as it moves in and out. Then I place my hands on or near my body wherever it hurts or wherever I want to put them. I then sit quietly for a bit. Sometimes my hands feel warm where they are touching my body. There are different hand places for different things."

He gave his tail a swish and continued, "This healing gift helps keep my mind, body, and spirit strong and healthy. It helps me stay balanced when I jump from branch to branch in the trees or leap over logs. It could help you with your hoppity-hop."

Hoppy said, "I would like to learn how to do this thing you call healing touch. Can you teach me?"

"I would love to teach you and your mommy and daddy," said Sam. "I have a class tonight after dinner."

Dad looked at Hoppy and said, "Let's do it so you can continue to get your hoppity-hop back."

That evening, after eating a yummy dinner, Hoppy's family went to the healing touch class. Sam, the teacher, had the class set up near the edge of the Healing Pond. The spot was perfect, since it had an open view of the pond for the students to watch Sam teach the class. It was a perfect little spot. The smell of the nearby Japanese honeysuckle made the spot even sweeter. Beautiful little white flowers called plantain pussytoes covered the shady areas under the trees. The leaves had a silvery white surface and looked like they were covered in white hair.

The class setup included small tree trunks and logs as seats that all seemed to face the pond. Penelope and Stevie also joined them for the class.

Sam started by teaching how the body is energy, thinking, feeling, and spirit. "You can't see the energy, but it is there," he told the class. "When you are not feeling like yourself or a bit yucky, sometimes your energy gets heavy and out of balance. When you do healing touch, you help your body's invisible waves of energy be calm and quiet. This helps you be well and heal faster."

Sam began to lead the class through an exercise. "Let's all start by taking a long slow breath in from your nose and then out from your mouth. This helps us be more focused. Now, move one hand and place it on your ankle, and put your other hand on your knee. We'll hold that position for one minute. Then move one of your hands to your knee and then the other hand to your hip. Keep following me. We will finish with one of your hands on your head and one facing up to the sky. This exercise helps calm the invisible energy waves of your body so it's just like a peaceful pond."

As Sam the squirrel showed the class where to place their hands, Hoppy laughed as he watched his mommy and daddy practice. Hoppy tried the hands still exercise, where he put both of his hands on his head, with one on his forehead and the other one on the back of his head. Hoppy was so calm that he gently fell off his tree-stump seat. He giggled and then got right back up and tried again. Hoppy was doing his best learning from his new friend Sam. He thought to himself, *This exercise seems very silly, but I do feel quieter in my mind!*

That night after the class, Hoppy drifted off to a deep sleep. He dreamt of playing hide-and-seek with his new friends near the Healing Pond, hiding behind the tall cattails and milkweed gently dancing in the breeze. His mind reminded him of the sweet smell of the Japanese honeysuckle. In his deep sleep, he took in a big breath to enjoy the sweet peaceful smell. He smiled, feeling joy in his heart. His mommy and daddy also slept well that night after practicing this new gift of healing touch that helped calm the body's energy. Gentle snoring sounds came from all directions in their tree-log home.

At breakfast the next day, Hoppy said, "I want to do the energy exercise again! That was fun, and I feel more balanced, just like my new friend Sam. Maybe today I can jump from tree branch to tree branch!"

Hoppy's mommy and daddy both smiled and laughed hearing Hoppy's plan for the day.

After finishing his breakfast, Hoppy was feeling strong, and he went out to play in the fresh air. He seemed to forget that once upon a time, he had lost his hoppity-hop! He hopped over tree branches on the forest floor and chased Monarch butterflies. He decided not to try jumping from branch to branch just yet. He thought, *One day, I will jump long and strong like the red-eyed tree frog and balance in the trees like my friend Sam the squirrel.*

Over the next few weeks, Hoppy and his mommy and daddy made visits with their new healing friends Sam the squirrel, Penelope the porcupine, and Stevie the skunk. Hoppy's mom decided to send a letter downstream to the holistic nurse to tell her the good news of Hoppy's healing.

In her letter, she wrote:

Dear Nurse Caitie,

We are so happy that you told us about the Healing Pond and about your friends with healing gifts. These gifts have helped Hoppy be stronger in his mind, body, and spirit. He has energy to play all day and is hungry again. Hoppy is on his way to getting his hoppity-hop back! We are so grateful for your holistic caring of Hoppy.

With thanks,
Hoppy's mommy

That afternoon, after a short nap, Hoppy's mommy and daddy packed a small picnic basket to take on a short hike. Along one of the winding paths, they came across a small friendly brown bear. He had round ears, a long snout, and shaggy hair. He was carrying a small wooden basket full of plants, berries, and flowers. He seemed to be looking for things on the forest floor.

Hoppy said, "Hello. My name is Hoppy, and this is my mommy and daddy."

The bear said, "My name is Bert. I live on the other side of the pond with my momma bear and my great-poppa bear."

Hoppy's mommy was looking at Bert's basket with curiosity. Bert explained that he had a healing gift. "I am a forager."

Hoppy asked, "What is a forager?"

Bert answered, "I pick berries and healing plants from the forest that help us stay healthy. The plants can help when we are feeling yucky or not like ourselves. Some of the wild plants in the forest are gifts for us to eat or make special drinks or syrups. My great-poppa bear showed me which plants to pick that are safe for us to eat. He also taught me that nature is wise. It teaches us about caring and healing. The plants nurture and protect each other. His wish is that I help teach others about the healing gifts of plants. My favorite berry is the elderberry. You can eat the berries cooked or make a yummy syrup to go on pancakes. My momma bear gives me elderberry syrup when I have a cough or to help me get better faster when I am getting a cold. I can teach you," Bert said.

"I would love to learn more about your healing gift of foraging," said Hoppy's mommy.

Over the next few weeks, Bert and Hoppy's mommy picked berries and healing plants like American ginseng and red clover. Bert taught her the names, shapes, colors, and healing gifts of each the berries and plants. He also showed her the best spots to forage and taught her what time of day and season to pick the plants.

Hoppy's mommy thought, *There is so much to learn from our new friend Bert. I will keep all my notes in my little plant book gifted to me by Bert's momma bear. Everyone has been so kind and caring, helping us get Hoppy's hoppity-hop back!*

Hoppy spent many of his mornings hopping and finding new paths around the pond. One day, as he hopped around the tall cattails and yellow root on the edge of the Healing Pond, he came upon a group of animals. There was a turtle, a fox, a dog, a squirrel, and an opossum. A black and white dog was teaching the group of animals different funny poses. They had their hands in the air, reaching up to the sun, then down on the ground, looking like a table. Then they were up again and then back down. They stretched with their arms, legs, and tails. It looked like a slow dance.

The yoga teacher invited Hoppy to come join the group. "Well, hello there, little frog," he said. "My name is Digby."

Hoppy asked, "What are you doing?"

Digby answered, "This healing gift is called yoga. Yoga helps each of us be healthy and in control of our breath and our response to our emotions. This helps us grow in our spirit. It can help us be more aware of everything around us."

Hoppy kept watching the class. The animals continued to rise and fall, reaching and stretching. They were all smiling and seemed happy.

"What do you call that pose?" Hoppy asked.

"It's my favorite one! Downward-facing dog," Digby answered.

"Can I try?" Hoppy asked.

"Of course you can!" said Digby.

Hoppy did his best, trying out the new stretches and poses.

"All yoga students should just do their best," Digby said.

Hoppy laughed quietly, thinking to himself, *Frogs and dogs have very different poses.*

When he got back home, Hoppy told his mommy and daddy that he had made a friend named Digby, and his healing gift was yoga. They chuckled. They were so happy to see their little boy making new friends at the Healing Pond.

Later that week, on a quiet afternoon, Stevie the skunk came to visit the frog family at their house. She brought Hoppy a new healing oil named lavender. "Lavender is a sweet-smelling oil that comes from lovely small purple flowers," she explained. "These flowers grow in different parts of the world, but you can grow them in your garden as well. My momma grows lavender in a beautiful sunny patch outside her kitchen window. When a small breeze passes through, we can smell it in our home."

She added, smiling at Hoppy, "A lavender bath is used for healing sore muscles after yoga—practicing new stretches and poses like downward-facing dog."

After dinner, Hoppy's daddy ran the water for a warm bath. He added some of the calming lavender oil that Stevie had given them. Hoppy's daddy then helped him safely into the tub. As Hoppy floated, he thought to himself, *This water is so warm and smells so peaceful.*

After drying him off from his soothing bath, his daddy tucked Hoppy in bed with his favorite green blankie and hugged him goodnight. Hoppy slept so well that night. He had sweet dreams of jumping from branch to branch of the tall mountain oak trees, balancing like his friend Sam.

When Hoppy woke up, he felt more peaceful, from practicing yoga with Digby the dog. After eating all his yummy pancakes with elderberry syrup, Hoppy wanted to practice his yoga. He started with the downward-facing dog pose. Hoppy giggled and said to his mommy and daddy, "This is such a silly pose for a frog!" His mommy laughed as she watched Hoppy twisting and turning into funny poses.

Each day was full of fun and learning. Hoppy practiced the energy medicine called healing touch to help with his mind, body, and spirit. He played by the Healing Pond and picked berries and healing plants with his mommy and his friend Bert the bear. Hoppy's mommy was so proud of her little frog for trying new things to help him get his hoppity-hop back.

That evening after dinner, the night air was cool and refreshing—perfect for a walk around the pond. Lovely green Christmas ferns and wild blue phlox covered the brown dirt floor of the forest. Small fallen branches, pine cones, and pine needles of many shades of brown were also part of the carpet woven by nature. There were tiny little blueberries hanging from some small shrubs nearby. Vines twisted their way up the trunks of trees, reaching for the sun. Each plant seemed to have a role in protecting or supporting the other.

As Hoppy and his daddy strolled down the path, they came upon a quiet spot. There was something special about this place. They sat down on a log that seemed to invite them to sit and be still. They took the time to simply listen with their hearts and their minds. In the quietness of the evening air, they heard the songs of crickets chirping from across the pond.

Suddenly, a voice came from the tree above. Hoppy looked up and saw a white feathery snowy owl perched on a branch. The owl had yellow eyes and a short black bill. His feet were covered with white feathers.

"Hello down there," said the owl. "My name is Ohm-Ar. Welcome to our Healing Pond."

"Hello," Hoppy answered.

The snowy owl gently clapped his wings in joy. "I see that you were invited to sit by the Welcome Log! How wise of you both to be quiet and still in your day, putting all your focus into each joyful breath. This is a good healing practice called mindfulness. A simple way to be quiet is to breathe in slowly, like you are smelling a flower. Then breathe out more slowly, like you are blowing out a candle. This healing breath helps us be more peaceful and makes our bodies stronger."

Hoppy's daddy thanked Ohm-Ar for his wise words and said that he would like to learn more about this gift of mindfulness.

The snowy owl nodded yes and said to Hoppy, "I have been watching you learn from your new friends. Our Healing Pond and the healing gifts help balance our feelings, our thinking, and our spirit. We just need to practice being still every day, just like when you practice yoga or healing touch. It is important to think about one breath and not about yesterday or tomorrow. Focus on being right here, right now, simply being and not trying. This is mindfulness. When I do this every day, I am more kind to myself and others and happier. It can help you with your mind, body, and spirit—and with your hoppity-hop."

Ohm-Ar then sat quietly on the branch practicing mindfulness. Hoppy and his daddy did the same as they continued to sit still, focusing on their breath. Once they both felt rested, they decided to head back home for the night. They waved goodnight to their new friend Ohm-Ar as they hopped down the path.

"I love the snowy owl's name. The sound Oohmm-Arrr vibrates in my body when I say it. His name is like music," Hoppy's daddy said.

Many days and weeks went by. Hoppy was hopping higher—nearly as high as some of the tall chickweed and the white turtlehead plants. At bedtime, he sipped the ginger tea that his mommy would make him. This made his belly feel good. He was now able to croak his evening song for all to hear. Ohm-Ar, the wise snowy owl, loved listening to his new little friend Hoppy sing his croaking songs in the evening as the sun went to sleep in the West.

Hoppy's mommy and daddy smiled as they watched Hoppy playing and getting stronger every day and croaking again. Moving upstream to the Healing Pond and meeting so many new friends with healing gifts was helping Hoppy get his hoppity-hop back.

Now Hoppy just hopped and hopped up and down over Christmas ferns, cleavers, and logs, hopping all day long on the forest floor. He had learned to hop high over the cleavers because the small seeds would stick to you like glue! Some days, he jumped from tree branch to tree branch like his friend Sam the squirrel. Practicing healing touch helped him be more balanced in everything he did.

Hoppy's mommy sent another note to the holistic nurse. She wrote:

Dear Nurse Caitie,

Hoppy is back! He is hopping everywhere. He is doing yoga with his friend Digby the dog and healing touch with Sam the squirrel. Bert the bear, a forager, and Hoppy pick berries and healing plants near the Healing Pond in these beautiful Blue Ridge Mountains.

Hoppy spends time listening to his wise friend Ohm-Ar the snowy owl and sitting still while practicing his mindfulness. Penelope the porcupine brings her special table to our home and places small quills on Hoppy when he is feeling yucky. Stevie, the aromatherapist, brings lovely-smelling oils to the house for all of us to enjoy. The oils help us be well and help with Hoppy's hoppity-hop.

Thank you for telling us about the Healing Pond and of the possible miracles from meeting your caring friends with all their healing gifts.

With love,
Hoppy's Mommy

One fine morning, after his usual breakfast, Hoppy asked his mommy and daddy to sit with him.

"I have a question," he said. "Now that my hoppity-hop is back, can we move back downstream when school is done? I would like to bring plants with healing gifts and plant flowers and berries around Frog Pond. I want to clean up the pond. I would also like to tell my friends how the gifts of healing touch, yoga, and aromatherapy can help us be happy and healthy. Can I also invite my new friend Ohm-Ar to come and share his gift of mindfulness, and Penelope her gift of acu … acup … acupunct … acupuncturrrr? I want all the other frogs to have their hoppity-hop back and hop, hop, hop all day long."

Hoppy's mommy and daddy gave him a big hug. "We are so happy and proud of you. Of course we can invite your new friends to Frog Pond. These healing gifts can help your friends be well and have their best hoppity-hop. The holistic nurse, Caitie the cat, will be so happy and just purr to see you hopping so high over all the big branches. Coming to the Healing Pond was such a gift and a healing journey for all our family."